TWO FINE SWINE

© Copyright 1994 by Kelli C. Foster, Gina C. Erickson, and Kerri Gifford

All inquiries should be addressed to:
Barron's Educational Series, Inc.
250 Wireless Boulevard
Hauppauge, NY 11788

International Standard Book Number 0-8120-1838-9

Library of Congress Catalog Card Number 93-38843

Library of Congress Cataloging-in-Publication Data

Foster, Kelli C.
    Two fine swine / by Foster & Erickson ; illustrations by Kerri
Gifford.
        p.   cm.—(Get ready—get set—read!)
        ISBN 0-8120-1838-9
        (1. Pigs—Fiction. 2. Valentines—Fiction. 3. Porcupines—Fiction.
4. Stories in ryme.) I. Erickson, Gina Clegg. II. Gifford, Kerri, ill. III. Title.
IV. Series: Erickson, Gina Clegg. Get ready—get set—read!
PZ7.F8155Val   1994
(E)—dc20   93-38843
                                                                                CIP
                                                                                AC

PRINTED IN HONG KONG
13 12 11 10 9 8

GET READY...GET SET...READ!

TWO FINE SWINE

by
Foster & Erickson

Illustrations by
Kerri Gifford

BARRON'S

Caroline and K.C. Swine
looked at the red and white
valentine.

"I wish it were mine,"
said Caroline.

"It is divine.
Let's go inside
and get in line."

Who will get the valentine?

"Nine, nine,
who has nine?"

K.C.'s eyes grew wide
and began to shine.

"The nine is mine!"
said K.C. Swine.

And with pride she took
the fine valentine.

Outside, they went for a ride.
They saw little Porcupine.

He was not fine.
He could not play.
He had to stay inside all day.

It did not take long
for them to decide.

They put it down
and ran to hide.

Mrs. Porcupine found it
and took it inside.

"Oh, is this pretty
valentine mine?"

Side by side, behind a
pine, K.C. and Caroline
began to shine.

The End

The INE Word Family

Caroline
divine
fine
line
mine
nine
pine
porcupine
shine
swine
valentine

The IDE Word Family

hide
ride
wide
pride
decide
inside
outside

Sight Words

eyes
grew
stay
were
took
behind
little
looked

Dear Parents and Educators:

Welcome to *Get Ready...Get Set...Read!*

We've created these books to introduce children to the magic of reading.

Each story in the series is built around one or two word families. For example, *A Mop for Pop* uses the OP word family. Letters and letter blends are added to OP to form words such as TOP, LOP, and STOP. As you can see, once children are able to read OP, it is a simple task for them to read the entire word family. In addition to word families, we have used a limited number of "sight words." These are words found to occur with high frequency in books your child will soon be reading. Being able to identify sight words greatly increases reading skill.

You might find the steps outlined on the facing page useful in guiding your work with your beginning reader.

We had great fun creating these books, and great pleasure sharing them with our children. We hope *Get Ready...Get Set...Read!* helps make this first step in reading fun for you and your new reader.

Kelli C. Foster, PhD
Educational Psychologist

Gina Clegg Erickson, MA
Reading Specialist

Guidelines for Using *Get Ready...Get Set...Read!*

Step 1.   Read the story to your child.

Step 2.   Have your child read the Word Family list aloud several times.

Step 3.   Invent new words for the list. Print each new combination for your child to read. Remember, nonsense words can be used (*dat, kat, gat*).

Step 4.   Read the story *with* your child. He or she reads all of the Word Family words; you read the rest.

Step 5.   Have your child read the Sight Word list aloud several times.

Step 6.   Read the story *with* your child again. This time he or she reads the words from both lists; you read the rest.

Step 7.   Your child reads the entire book to you!

There are five sets of books in the

Series. Each set consists of five **FIRST BOOKS**
and two **BRING-IT-ALL-TOGETHER BOOKS**.

SET 1

is the first set your children should read.
The word families are selected from the short vowel sounds:
at, **ed**, **ish** and **im**, **op**, **ug**.

SET 2

provides more practice
with short vowel sounds:
an and **and**, **et**, **ip**, **og**, **ub**.

SET 3

focuses on
long vowel sounds:
ake, **eep**, **ide** and **ine**, **oke** and **ose**, **ue** and **ute**.

SET 4

introduces the idea that the word family sounds
can be spelled two different ways:
ale/ail, **een/ean**, **ight/ite**, **ote/oat**, **oon/une**.

SET 5

acquaints children with word families that
do not follow the rules for long and short vowel sounds:
all, **ound**, **y**, **ow**, **ew**.